Crazy Miss M Alphabet Pets

Contents

For my brother, Steve, who put up with my pets long after they were overdue!

Chapter 1

Down a quiet street in a quiet part of town lived Miss Maisey, who looked rather crazy. Her hair stuck up like a rooster's and her clothes were grasshopper green.

Miss Maisey was once a school librarian, but now she owned the most unusual pet shop ever. Outside, it looked ordinary. However, inside, it was most *extraordinary*.

The pet shop was a cross between a jungle and a library. Luckily, Miss Maisey knew exactly where everything was. She filed the pets in alphabetical order.

The apes and aardvarks
and other animals beginning
with *A* roamed near the front
of the shop, while the zebras
and zebus grazed towards
the back. In between were
all the other pets of the alphabet.

Chapter 2

In another part of town lived a boy
named Billy, who wanted to get
a fun pet. So, one day, he went
to Miss Maisey's shop. Once he'd
crashed his way to the counter,
he asked if he could buy a pet.

"No way!" cried Miss Maisey.
"Oh..." said Billy.
"I don't *sell* pets," barked
Miss Maisey, in a very librarian
voice. "I *lend* them!"

Billy's face lit up.

"Great! Can I borrow
a kangaroo?" he asked.

"Impossible!" Miss Maisey
squawked. "You have to start
at the beginning of the alphabet.
I've got aardvarks, alligators,
antelopes, apes, and, just returned
today, an army of ants."

"Ummm, I'll take out an alligator, please," said Billy.

Miss Maisey got Billy to write his name and address on a card in his best writing, then she stamped it with the date when the alligator was due back.

❰ Chapter 3 ❱

When Billy and the alligator got home, they went for a swim and started to have fun. They splished and splashed in the pool until nearly all the water had spilled out.

When Billy's mother saw what was going on, she cried, "Stop, stop! Take it back to the shop!"

So Billy returned the alligator.
He put it in the Returns box,
which already had a crocodile in it.

Then Billy went to the counter.

"Can I borrow a bear now?" asked Billy.

"Sorry, it's been taken out," explained Miss Maisey. "How about a bat?"

"Yes, *please*!" cried Billy.

Billy and the bat raced home
to have fun. They did everything
upside down.

They swung upside down in the
trees. They walked upside down.

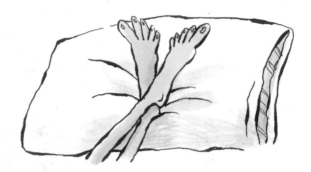

That night, Billy even slept
upside down! His feet were where
his head should have been.

When Billy's mother saw what was going on, she cried, "Stop, stop! Take it back to the shop!"

So, early the next morning,
once he'd eaten breakfast
standing on his head,
Billy went back to the pet shop.
"Now I'd like a chimpanzee,
please," said Billy, handing back
the bat.

Miss Maisey made her way over to the C section – past the oversized area where the camels and caribou were filed – and brought back a chimpanzee.

After he'd had his card stamped, Billy left the shop.

It wasn't long before they started
to have fun. They played on
the swing in the backyard. They
swung up and over, up and over,
until they felt very dizzy.

When Billy's mother saw what
was going on, she cried, "Stop, stop!
Take it back to the shop!"

19

Chapter 4

A couple of days later, Billy's mother still didn't like any of the pets that Billy had brought home.

The dingo howled along to songs on the radio.

The elephant romped and stomped
in jumbo-sized puddles.

And the fox played "chicken"
from dawn till dusk.

Every time, Billy's mother cried,
"Stop, stop! Take it back to the shop!"

She said the same thing when
the gorilla skated on banana skins,

the horse jumped over chairs
and down stairs,

the iguana sunbathed
by the pool all day long,

the jackrabbit jived the jitterbug,

and the kangaroo played
peek-a-boo.

Chapter 5

By now, Billy was feeling sad.
He was nearly halfway through the
alphabet, and he *still* couldn't find
a pet. The lizards, which were next
in the alphabet, had been taken out
by a girl doing a science display.

Since Billy didn't like moles or
numbats, he asked if he could go
straight to *O*. Miss Maisey agreed,
but only after she made Billy
recite his alphabet, forwards
and backwards.

At last, Billy was happy.
He thought an octopus,
with its eight long arms,
would be good at throwing balls.

However, the octopus was hopeless. Its arms kept getting tangled into knots. When it finally tossed some balls, they hit the man from next door.

When Billy's mother saw
what was going on, she cried,
"Stop, stop! Take it back
to the shop!"

⟨ Chapter 6 ⟩

By now, Miss Maisey was feeling down, too. She hadn't had anyone go as far as this down the alphabet in order to find a suitable pet.

She didn't stock that many
P, *Q*, or *R* pets. There was
a porcupine, but everyone usually
returned it the same day. It had
a prickly personality! The quail was
feeling rather frail, and the racoon
was booked to go out by noon.

A retired snake charmer had
just taken the last of her snakes.
He wanted to see if he still
had his charm.

There was a tiger from Sumatra,
hiding in the tall grass in the *Rare
Pets* area of the *T* section, but Billy
explained to Miss Maisey that tiger
fur made his mother sneeze.

There was even a unicorn
in an area known as *The Fable
Stables*. It walked in the wild with
the yetis and dragons. But Billy
had never really liked fantasy.

Miss Maisey suggested that he skip past the *V* and *W* animals. She didn't think they would be much fun at all.

"The vultures only want to eat," she explained, "and the wolves are kind of the same."

"What about an *X* pet then?" asked Billy, hopefully.

"There aren't any," she said. "Well... there's a Xenopus, a clawed toad, but no one's ever requested one. I could reserve one for you."

But Billy couldn't wait that long.

He finally settled on a yak. Miss Maisey let Billy have it out for an extra week since he was having so much trouble finding the right pet.

Then Billy and the yak headed home to have fun, and that's when the trouble *really* started.

The yak talked non-stop. It went
yakkety-yakkety-yak to everyone
along the way. It would have
talked the hind leg off a donkey,
given the chance.

So, when Billy's mother heard
what was going on, she cried,
"Stop, stop! Take it back to the shop!"

Billy's mother had just about
had enough. She lay on the sofa
with an ice-bag on her head
and cucumber slices over her eyes.

"I can't stop now! I've only
got *Z* to go," said Billy.

"I've got a headache. Zebra
stripes would turn it into
a migraine!" cried Billy's mother.

"Then what pet can I get?"
asked Billy.

"Something that's very, very
q-u-i-e-t," she whispered.

Chapter 7

Early the next day, Billy raced
to Miss Maisey's. He told her
that his mother wanted him
to get a very, very quiet pet.

"Oh, that'll be in the basement
in the *Extra*ordinary section,"
she explained. "It may take me
a while to find a quiet, ordinary pet.
We don't have much call for those!"

A long, long time later,
Miss Maisey came back holding
a plastic bag with a tadpole in it.

"If I like this pet, can I get
an extension on it?" asked Billy.

"Certainly, but I don't think you'll
need it!" said Miss Maisey, winking
at him and laughing like a hyena.

Mrs

"Thank you," he said, thinking
that Miss Maisey was really
a little crazy. He left the shop,
carrying his tadpole in its plastic
bag full of water and pondweed.

Billy slowly strolled home, because he didn't think the tadpole would be much fun at all.

By the time he got home, however, Billy had started to like his plain tadpole. He enjoyed watching it splash and dash through the water.

At last, Billy's mother was happy.
She was glad that Billy had found
a pet that didn't hang upside down,
or throw balls at the neighbour.

For the next few weeks, Billy rushed home every day after school and just sat in the living room, watching his tadpole go around and around and around in circles.

Billy was glad that his mother had made him get a plain, quiet, ordinary pet.

But then, just when Billy least expected it...

the quiet little tadpole turned
into a toad that played leapfrog
in the living room!

A voice cried, "Stop, stop!
Take it back to the shop!"

Only this time, it was Billy's!

From the Author

 Wild horses couldn't have
stopped me from going
to Miss Maisey's pet shop.
My mother wanted me
to have plain pets, too. But, one dog
and three cats later, I think she would
have liked a pet shop like Miss Maisey's.
That way, she could have put them
all back in the Returns box!

Janine Scott

 # From the Illustrator

 I used to think librarians were
quiet, ordinary people, but
after creating the illustrations
of Miss Maisey and meeting
the amazing animals in her lending
library of pets... well, I'm not so sure
any more!

Sandr